Chinese Word Writing

寫字課本

Initial Edition 起步版

2

Min Guo
郭敏

U0130742

香港字藝出版社
Hong Kong Word Art Press

Chinese Word Writing 2 (*Initial Edition*)　　A Series of Textbooks of Chinese U See

Illustrator:　Min Guo
Published by　Hong Kong Word Art Press
Editor:　Jin-li Li
Address:　Unit 503, 5/F, Tower 2, Lippo Center, 89 Queensway Road, Admiralty, HK
Website:　www.wordart.com.hk/www.chineseusee.com
Edition:　Second edition published in April, 2016, Hong Kong
Size:　215 mm x 270 mm
ISBN:　978-988-14915-3-4

寫字課本 2 （起步版）　　象形卡通系列教科書

作　　者：郭　敏
繪　　畫：郭　敏
編　　輯：李金麗
出　　版：香港字藝出版社
地　　址：香港金鐘金鐘道 89 號力寶中心第 2 座 5 樓 503 室
網　　頁：www.wordart.com.hk/www.chineseusee.com
版　　次：2016 年 4 月香港第二版第一次印刷
規　　格：215 mm x 270 mm
國際書號：978-988-14915-3-4

Table of Contents
目錄

1

Lesson One
第一課

I/me

    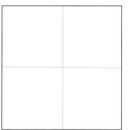

nǐ

you

   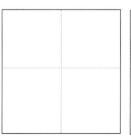 

tā

他

he/him

    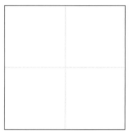

tā

她

she/her

   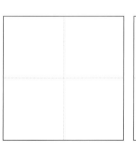 

tā

it (animal)

    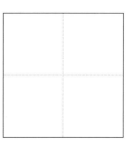

shé

snake

    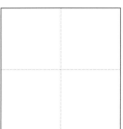

shì

be/is/am/are

   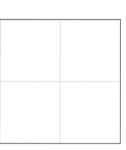 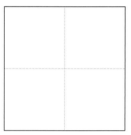

Trace the following cartoon and write out the related word. 塗描下列卡通，並寫出相應的漢字。

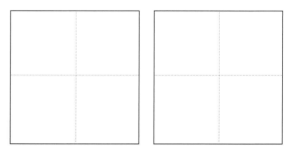

1. Write out the word to each cartoon. 看圖寫字。

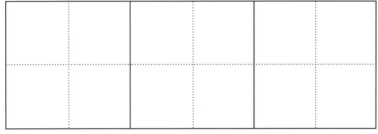

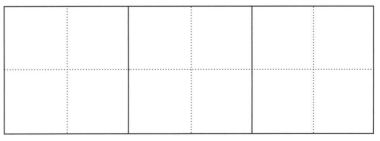

2. Trace the following words. 塗描下列各字。

我 蟲 蛇
他 牠 是 你
羔 她 也

3. Complete the following sentences. 完成下列各句。

她不是

他也不是

你不是

我也不是

牠是

4. Find the same parts and the relationship among the following cartoons and then write them out on the lines. 找出下列卡通相同的部份及它們之間的聯繫，並寫字下面的橫線上。

1)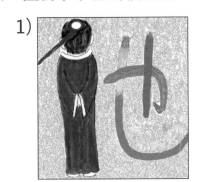

2)

3)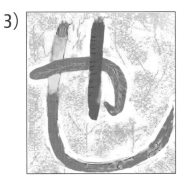

4)

5)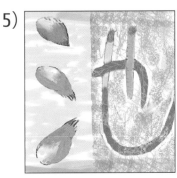

6)

jiě

姐

elder sister

chí

池

pool

chí

馳

gallop

_____

_____

_____

_____

_____

_____

_____

5. Trace the following cartoon and write out the related word. 塗描下列卡通，並寫出相應的漢字。

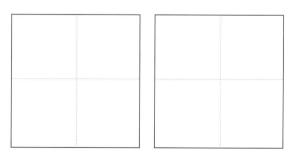

2

Lesson Two
第二課

men

plural

 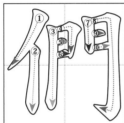 

de

of/a suffix

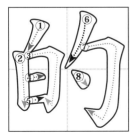 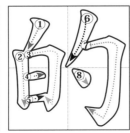 

nǚ

female/woman

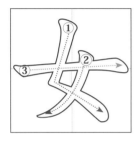  

lì

labour/strength/
power

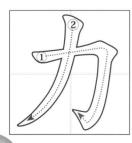  

hái

children/child

   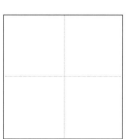 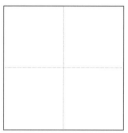

lǎo

old/senior

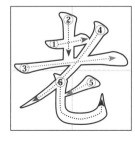   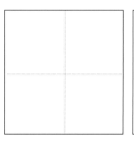 

mén

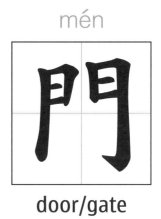

門

door/gate

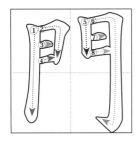 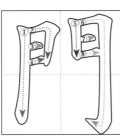 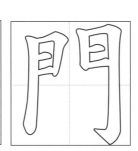 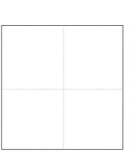 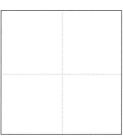

tián

田

farmland/field

lì

力

labour/strength/
power

nán

男

male/man

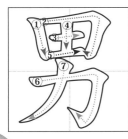    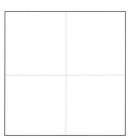

zǐ

子

son

xiǎo

系

small/little

sūn

孫

grandson

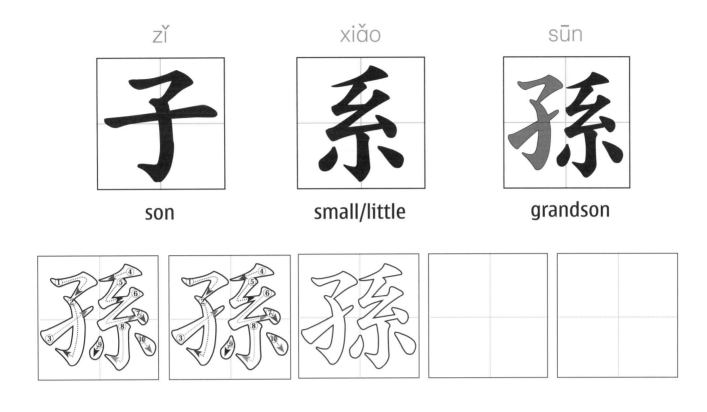

gǒu

狗

dog

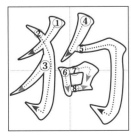 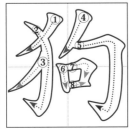   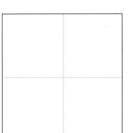

sháo

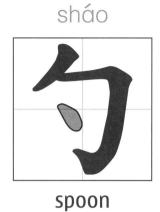

spoon

jù

sentence

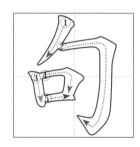 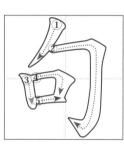  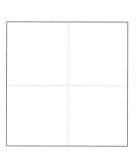 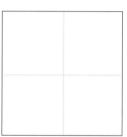

Trace the following cartoon and write out the related word. 塗描下列卡通，並寫出相應的漢字。

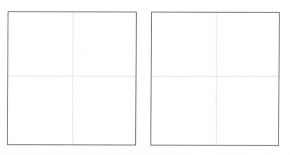

1. Write out the word to each cartoon. 看圖寫字。

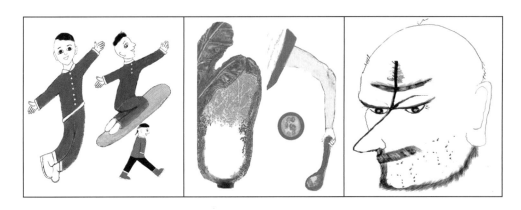

2. Trace the following words. 塗描下列各字。

3. Translate the following Chinese into English. 漢譯英。

老人 _____

小孩 _____

小狗 _____

男人 _____

女人 _____

4. Read the following passage. 閱讀下列短文。

門口有一條大狗，一隻燕子飛過來，大狗說：「早上好！」

燕子問：「你好，老兄，你看見我的孩子們沒有？」

天上飛着幾隻小鳥。 大狗說：「那幾隻小鳥，是嗎？」

「那就是我的兒子、女兒和孫子們。再見了，老兄！」說完，燕子飛走了。

Guess the answers to the following questions. 猜一猜下列問題的答案

1) 誰在門口？

_____

2) 誰有孩子？

_____

3) 誰會飛？

_____

4) 小鳥在哪裏飛？

_____

5) 大狗有孫子嗎？

_____

6) 故事發生在上午還是下午(Is the story happening in the morning or in the afternoon）？

_____

5. Trace the following cartoon and write out the related word. 塗描下列卡通，並寫出相應的漢字。

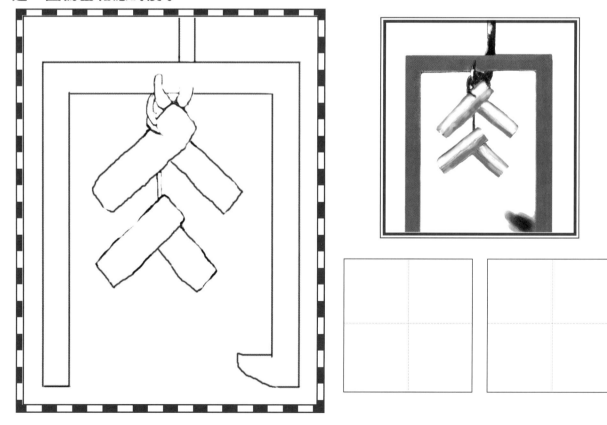

3

Lesson Three
第三課

zhè

this

   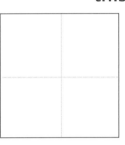 

nà

that

   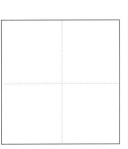 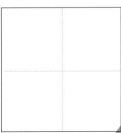

19

shuí/shéi

who/whom

   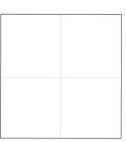 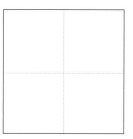

zài

exist/in/on/at

   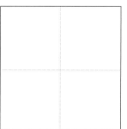 

nǎ

where

lǐ

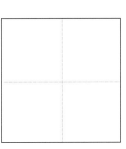 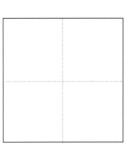

inner/inside

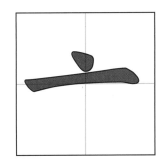   

    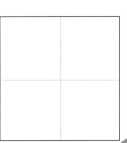

21

wén

culture/
a language

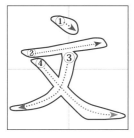 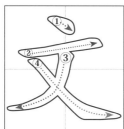 

shī

teacher/advisor

    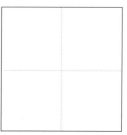

kǒu

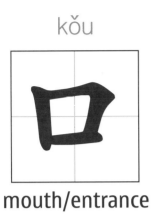

mouth/entrance

rén

people

qiú

prisoner

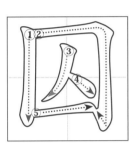 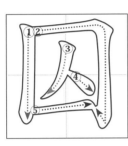   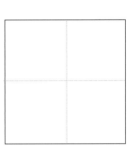

kǒu

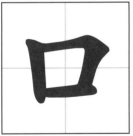

mouth/entrance

mù

wood

kùn

imprisoned/
difficult

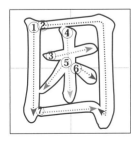 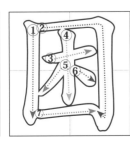 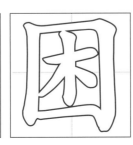  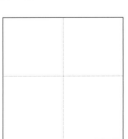

23

mén

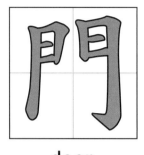

door

kǒu

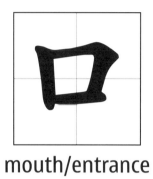

mouth/entrance

wèn

ask

 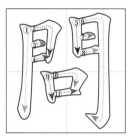  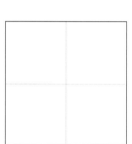 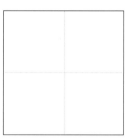

mén

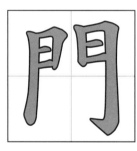

door

rì

sun

jiān

between

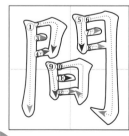   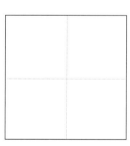 

1. Write out the word to each cartoon. 看圖寫字。

2. Trace the following words. 塗描下列漢字。

3. Translate the following Chinese into English. 漢譯英。

大門
_____

老師
_____

哪裏
_____

牛肉
_____

門口
_____

4. Change the following sentences into questions like the example.
　參照例子將下列句子變成問句。

例 (e.g.)：這是我的老師。⟶　這是誰?

1) 那是我媽媽。

_____

2) 他們在這裏。

_____

3) 這個人是小文。

_____

4) 他是我哥哥。

_____

5) 我是王玉。

_____

6) 小鳥在那裏。

_____

5. Guess the meanings of the words according to the cartoons. 看圖
猜字。

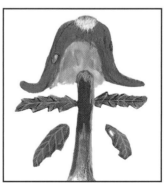

6. **Draw a line between the radicals and the words.** 將正確的偏旁和字用線連起來。

孩　蝶　家　什　海　們　洋　皂　蝴　安
蛇　汰　他　的　孫　伯　河　仙　蜥　好

7. **Trace the following cartoon and write out the related word.** 塗描下列卡通，並寫出相應的漢字。

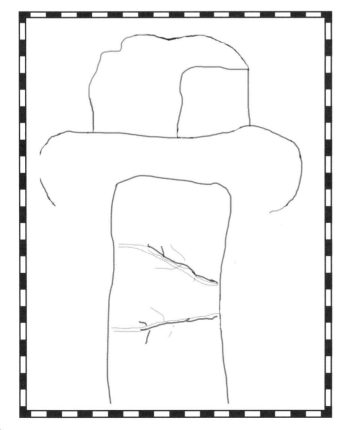

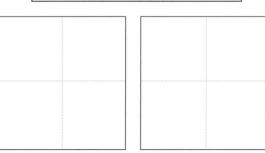

4

Lesson Four
第四課

xī

夕

sunset

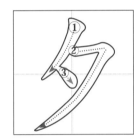 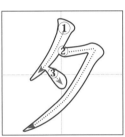  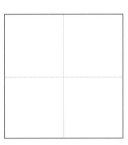 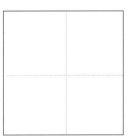

jiào

叫

call/bark

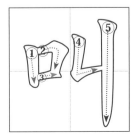 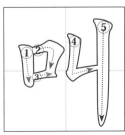   

nián

year

  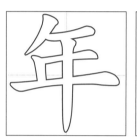

xìng

surname

jīn

today/now

   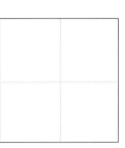 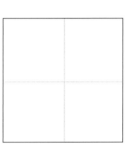

lǐ

a surname

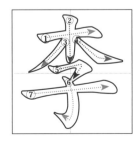    

31

kuài

quick/fast

zhǐ

stop

Wu Radical

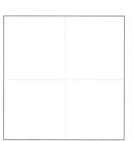

a component

suì

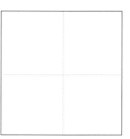

years old/age

1. Write sentences with the following words. 用下列漢字造句。

姓名 _____

出生 _____

歲   _____

屬   _____

鼠 shǔ	牛 niú	虎 hǔ	兔 tù	龍 lóng	蛇 shé
馬 mǎ	羊 yáng	猴 hóu	雞 jī	狗 gǒu	豬 zhū

2. Make a birthday card like the following example. 參照例子畫一張生日卡。

It can also be done by stickers. 這張生日卡也可以用小貼紙做。

3. Find the meanings of the following phrases in a dictionary by pinyin. 根據拼音在字典中查出下列成語的意思。

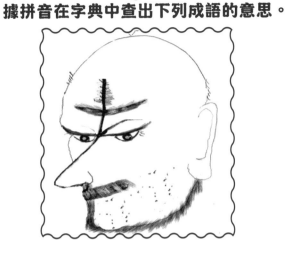

lǎo jiān jù huá

1) 老 奸 巨 猾

_____

_____

hú jiǎ hǔ wēi

2) 狐 假 虎 威

_____

_____

wáng yáng bǔ láo

3) 亡 羊 補 牢

_____

_____

shǒu zhū dài tù

4) 守 株 待 兔

_____

_____

4. Draw the following word cartoons like the example. 參照例子畫出下列卡通。

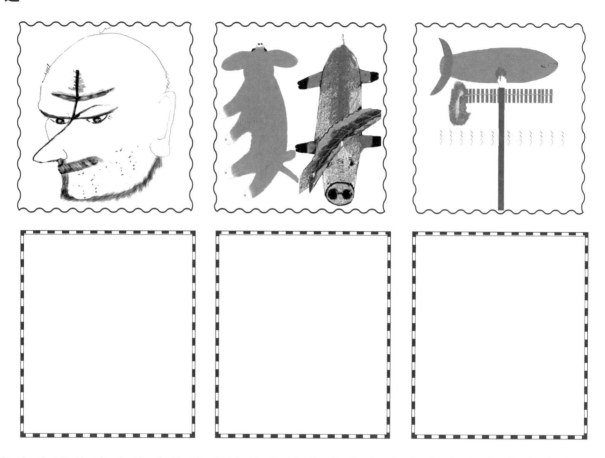

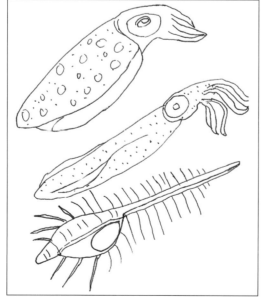

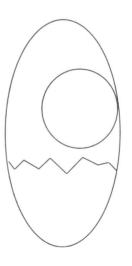

5

Lesson Five
第五課

jiě/zǐ

elder sister

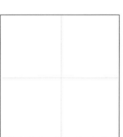
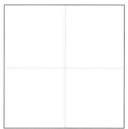

gē

elder brother

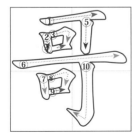

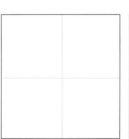
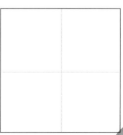

jiā

home/family

    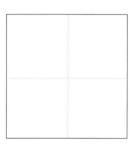

yǒu

have/there be

mā

媽

mother

  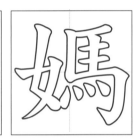 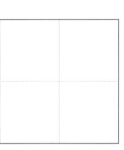 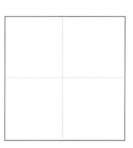

bà

爸

father

    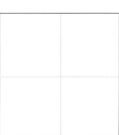

hé

and/with

qiě

且

moreover

bā

巴

jaw

mǎ

馬

horse

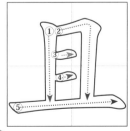 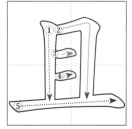 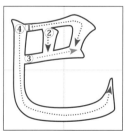  

míng

name

zì

word

bù/bú

no/not

    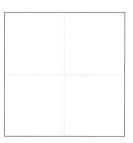

méi/mò

have not/sink

1. Write out the word to each cartoon. 看圖寫字。

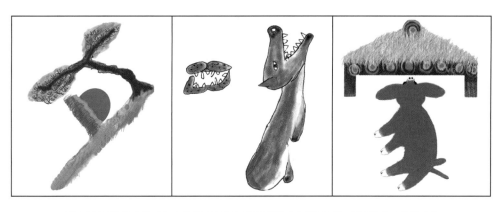

2. Trace the following words. 塗描下列各字。

3. Translate the following English into Chinese. 英譯漢。

1) This is my elder sister.

_____

2) That is my elder brother.

_____

3) My father and mother are over there.

_____

4) I have two elder sisters and one elder brother.

_____

5) There are five people in his family.

_____

4. Read the following passage. 閱讀下列短文。

大白鵝家人口眾多。家裏有爸爸、媽媽和七個孩子。

鵝媽媽叫牠大女兒一聲「鵝」， 叫牠二女兒兩聲「鵝」， 叫牠三女兒三聲「鵝」； 鵝爸爸叫牠大兒子一聲「鵝」， 叫牠二兒子兩聲「鵝」， 叫牠三兒子三聲「鵝」， 叫牠四兒子四聲「鵝」。 鵝媽媽和鵝爸爸叫很多聲「鵝」，就是叫牠們所有的孩子， 因為牠們都沒有名字， 大哥、 小弟、 大姐和小妹都叫「鵝」。

New words 生詞：

聲：sound   所有的：all of   因為：because   都：all

Guess the answers to the following questions. 猜一猜下列問題的答案。

1) 大白鵝家有幾口人？

_____

2) 牠們都叫甚麼名字？

_____

3) 大白鵝有幾個女兒？

_____

4) 大白鵝有幾個兒子？

_____

5) 大白鵝怎樣叫牠的三女兒？

_____

5. Trace the following cartoon and write out the related word. 塗描下列卡通，並寫出相應的漢字。

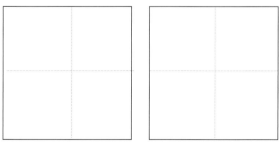

6

Lesson Six
第六課

fù

senior

a sound radical

yé

grandfather

   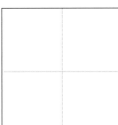

nǎi

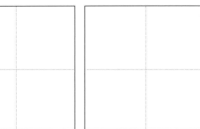

grandmother

   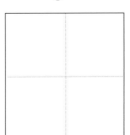 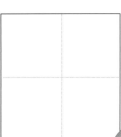

mèi

younger sister

dì

younger brother

gōng

male/old man

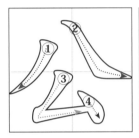 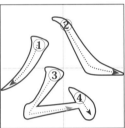   

pó

old lady

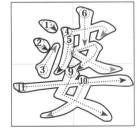 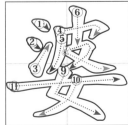 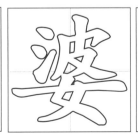  

wài

outside

 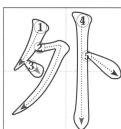  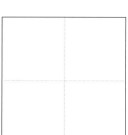 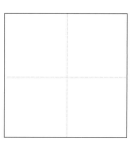

nǎi

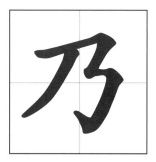

be (formal)

jí

and (formal)

 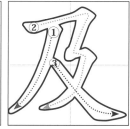  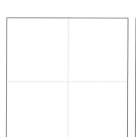 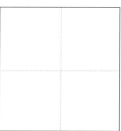

mù

wood

běn

root/book

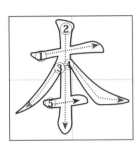 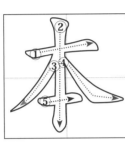   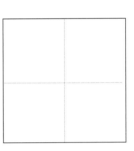

běn

root/book

mò

end

    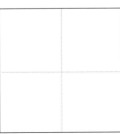

mò

end

wèi

not yet/future

    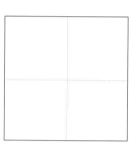

Draw the word cartoon like the example and write out the word. 參照例子畫出下面的卡通，並寫出相應的漢字。

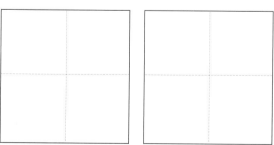

1. Write out the word to each cartoon. 看圖寫字。

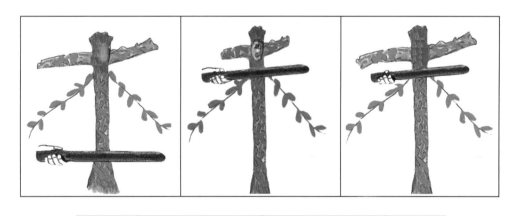

2. Trace the following words. 塗描下列各字。

爺 奶 妹
弟 有 婆 公
外 末 未

3. Match the words with the cartoons. 字畫相配。

1)	2)	3)	4)	5)
zhú	zhòng	niǎo	chū	guī
竹	種	鳥	出	龜
bamboo	plant	bird	out	turtle

A

B

C

D

E

F

4. Read the following passage. 閱讀下列短文。

　　一個老爺爺住在森林裏。一天，從他種的大西瓜裏爬出來一個小男孩兒。小男孩兒叫他：「爺爺，爺爺！」

　　「我不是你爺爺。」

　　小孩兒又叫：「姥爺，姥爺！」

　　「我也不是你姥爺。」老爺爺說。

　　「那我叫您甚麼呢？」小孩問。

　　「你是誰家的孩子？」老爺爺問。

　　「我是您的孩子。」小孩兒說。

　　「甚麼？」老爺爺問。

　　「我是從您種的西瓜裏出來的。」小孩兒說。

　　「那，那你就叫我老爺爺吧！」

　　小孩子成了老爺爺的家人。在老爺爺生日的那一天，小男孩兒叫來森林裏的小鳥，竹林裏的小蟲子和水裏的小烏龜。牠們一起在老爺爺的門口唱歌，給老爺爺慶祝生日。

New words 生詞：

出來：come out　成了：become　唱歌：sing a song

Guess the answers to the following questions. 猜一猜下列問題的答案。

1) 小男孩是從哪裏出來的？

2) 小男孩兒是誰家的孩子？

_____

3) 老爺爺是不是爺爺？

_____

4) 在老爺爺生日的那天，小男孩兒叫來了誰？

_____

5) 牠們在哪裏唱歌？

_____

5. Translate the following English into Chinese. 英譯漢。

1) Grandfather on your mother's side.

_____

2) Grandmother on your father's side.

_____

3) Your second elder sister.

_____

4) Your parents.

_____

6. Trace the following cartoon and write out the related word. 塗描下列卡通，並寫出相應的漢字。

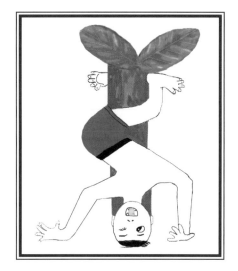

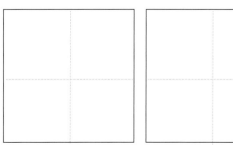

7. Create your family album like the example. 參照例子做一個家庭相冊，例（e.g.）：媽。

 →

這是我媽媽，她今年四十歲。她的名字叫王玉。

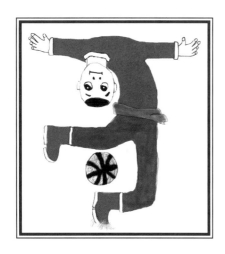

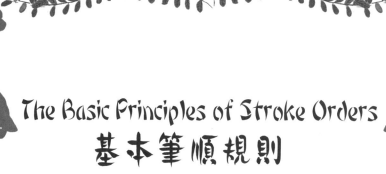

The Basic Principles of Stroke Orders
基本筆順規則

1)	先橫後豎	Draw the horizontal stroke first, then draw the vertical stroke.
2)	先撇後捺	Draw the left-falling stroke first, then draw the right-falling stroke.
3)	先上後下	Draw from the top strokes down to the bottom strokes.
4)	從左到右	Draw from the left strokes to the right strokes.
5)	先中間後兩邊	Draw the middle strokes before drawing the strokes at the sides.
6)	先外後裏	Draw from the outside strokes to the inside strokes.
7)	先裏後封口	Draw the inside strokes and then close the "door".
8)	點在上或左邊先寫	If a dot is on the top and the left, draw it first.
9)	點在下或右邊后寫	If a dot is on the bottom and the right, draw it last.